Disney
Winnie the Pooh

A Hundred-Acre Wood Storybook

D1450191

Based on the "Winnie the Pooh" works by A.A. Milne and E.H. Shepard

Stories by Kathleen W. Zoehfeld
Illustrations by Robbin Cuddy

Printed in China

ISBN 1-4231-0557-5

Winnie the Pooh

A Hundred-Acre Wood Storybook

Disney PRESS

New York

Contents

Pooh's First Day of School

"School is starting! School is starting!" cried Tigger. "Come on! Don't be late!"

"School?" asked Winnie the Pooh. "What are you talking about?"

"Christopher Robin has a new backpack and lunch box, and he's getting ready for school. We better get ready, too!" Tigger said.

"Oh Tigger," said Pooh. "School is for children. Not for fluff and stuffing like us."

Tigger and Pooh decided to tell the news to the rest of their friends.

". . . So school is starting," Tigger finished explaining. "And tiggers LOVE to go to school."

"Piglets don't love school," said Piglet thoughtfully. "At least I don't think we do."

"You're right, Piglet," said Eeyore. "This schooling business—pencils and whatnot—is overrated if you ask me."

"I think it sounds great!" cried little Roo. "Can I go, too?"

"Come along, Roo," said Pooh. "We'll all go and see Christopher Robin. Maybe he can tell us more about it."

Tigger was the first to bound through Christopher Robin's door. "Okay, where's the school?" he asked.

"It's about a mile away," said Christopher Robin. "The school bus will come tomorrow morning to take me there."

"A mile?" asked Piglet, pulling his ear.

"It's not here in the Hundred-Acre Wood?" asked Tigger.

"If you have to go that far from home, I'm sure school is not a good thing for piglets," said Piglet.

"We don't have the brains for it, anyway," said Pooh.

"You'd all like school," said Christopher Robin. "I'm sure you would. Wait right here a minute, and I'll make a classroom just for us."

"Imagine, our very own school!" said Pooh. "I wonder if we're up to it."

"Can we bounce in school?" asked Roo.

"Of course you can, Little Buddy!" said Tigger. "School's the bounciest place there is!"

"Oh no! There's no bouncing in school," said Eeyore decisively.

"None?" asked Tigger.

"School is work. There's no time for fun," said Eeyore.

"Not even a little?" asked Tigger. His shoulders drooped.

Eeyore shook his head knowingly.

"Oh," said Tigger, in a very small voice for a tigger. "Maybe tiggers don't like school after all."

He and Piglet were about to tiptoe away when Christopher Robin called out, "Time for school to begin!"

"Oh d-dear," said Piglet.

Christopher Robin set up a table, and around it he put chairs just the right size for his friends.

"We always sing a song first," said Christopher Robin as they gathered around. "*Good morning to Tigger, good morning to Roo. Welcome, all children, good morning to you!* Now everyone join in!"

"This is fun, Piglet. Don't you think?" whispered Pooh.

"Shhh," said Piglet.

"*Good morning,*" they all sang.

"If it is a good morning," said Eeyore, "which I doubt."

"Well, the first morning at school can be hard," said Christopher Robin. "But I've met my new teacher, and I know she's really nice. And I know two friends who will be in my class."

"It is friendly to spend your days with friends," said Piglet.

"And we learn things in school, too," said Christopher Robin.

"That may be okay for you," said Pooh. "But we're nothing but stuffing. Do you really think a little schooling will improve us?"

"Sure," said Christopher Robin. "You can learn to write your ABC's. It's fun."

Christopher Robin handed out paper and crayons. "Let's all draw pictures of ourselves."

"What does that have to do with ABC's?" asked Tigger.

"The best letters of the alphabet are the letters in our own names," said Christopher Robin. "When our pictures are finished, we can write our names on them."

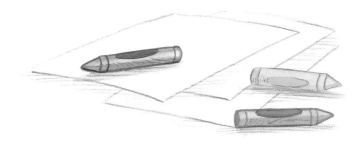

Pooh picked up a purple crayon.
"P-O-O-H," he said as he slowly
printed his name.

"Very nice!" cried Christopher
Robin.

"P-T," wrote Piglet, whose name
was really quite complicated.

Eeyore, who only knew the
letter A, wrote "A" under his
picture. "Don't know when I've had so much fun," he
said proudly.

Then Roo made some quotation marks.

And Tigger made a squiggle.

Everyone did a fine job.

"Counting is easy, too," said Christopher Robin. "Pooh, let's see how high you can stack these blocks."

"One, two, three, four, five, six," Pooh counted.

It was turning into a lovely tower. But when tiggers see towers, they think, towers are for bouncing, and—

Crash! Down went the blocks.

"Oh," said Pooh with a sigh.

"Tig-ger!" said Christopher Robin sternly.

"Sorry," said Tigger. "All these ABC's and 1-2-3's are fine, but what about fun? What good is a place if you can't even bounce in it?"

"It's true, you can't bounce when your teacher is talking," said Christopher Robin, "but my school has a playground, and we get to go outside and play nearly every day."

"A real playground?" asked Roo.

"Yes," said Christopher Robin. "A real playground with slides and swings and everything."

"I knew tiggers loved school!" cried Tigger.

But Pooh, whose tummy was beginning to feel a bit rumbly, was worried about something else.

"I hope you're allowed to eat at school," he said.

"Oh yes," said Christopher Robin. "That's what my new lunch box is for. I'm going to take a peanut-butter-and-honey sandwich, a banana, and milk."

 "Mmmm," Pooh said wistfully.

And then Christopher Robin, who knew his friend very well, said, "Why don't we have a little snack right now?"

He set out a large pot of honey, and everyone had a taste.

"Christopher Robin, I hope your new teacher is as nice as you are," said Piglet.

"Yes!" agreed Pooh. "Can we play again tomorrow?"

"Please!" everyone cried.

"Of course," said Christopher Robin. "We'll play every day—as soon as I get home from school."

Pooh Helps Out

Winnie the Pooh sat on the edge of his bed and looked all around his cozy house. There's nothing to do, he thought.

Pooh tried humming a little hum. "Hum de dum," he hummed. "Well, that's a nothing little hum," he said.

After a while, nothing to do began to feel quite bothersome. So he decided to get dressed.

Maybe I should find someone to do nothing with, he thought. That would be so much more cheerful.

Pooh went to Piglet's house and knocked on his door. "Piglet," he said, "I've come to see if you'd like to do nothing with me."

"Oh, I'd like to do nothing," said Piglet, "but first I have to wash my dishes."

Pooh brightened. "Oh, may I help?" he asked.

"Yes, indeed!" cried Piglet. He handed Pooh a towel. Piglet washed and Pooh dried.

When all the dishes were stacked neat and clean in the cupboard, Piglet said, "Thank you, Pooh. That was the perfect chore for two. Now I'm ready to do nothing."

Pooh hummed. Piglet wiggled his ears and tapped his foot.

Pooh yawned. Then Piglet had to yawn, too.

"Pooh?" Piglet said. "Are you having a lot of fun?"

"No," said Pooh thoughtfully, "doing nothing is NOT a lot of fun."

"I was thinking," said Piglet, "maybe somebody needs us to help them with something."

"Something would be much better than nothing," agreed Pooh.

"Let's ask Owl," said Piglet. And with that, Pooh and Piglet set off for Owl's tree house.

"Owl!" called Pooh. "Do you need us to help you?"

"Most certainly!" declared Owl. "This dusting will get done more quickly with the help of two good friends."

Pooh and Piglet loved Owl's feather dusters—they were great for tickling and cleaning.

"Thank you," said Owl, when his home was tidy and clean. "Now I'm free to do nothing."

So Owl looked out of his window. Pooh counted his paws, but that didn't take long. And Piglet shifted in his seat.

"Maybe Tigger needs our help with something," suggested Piglet.

The three friends decided to go to Tigger's house.

"Tigger!" called Pooh. "Do you need us to help you?"

"You're just the guys I wanted to see!" cried Tigger. "Picking up my toys would be much easier with three friends to help."

Piglet put away the toys on the lowest shelf. Pooh and Owl put away the toys on the middle shelves. And Tigger bounced up high to put away the toys on the top shelf.

"We're a great team!" cried Tigger. "Let's go see if Eeyore needs anything picked up."

"Eeyore!" called Pooh.

"Oh!" everyone gasped. Eeyore's house had fallen down.

"It's much better as a house when it's upright," said Eeyore.

"What happened?" asked Pooh.

"Just what usually happens," said Eeyore. "The wind blew it down."

"Well," said Pooh, "it looks as if you could use some help."

So Pooh, Piglet, Owl, and Tigger helped Eeyore put his house together again. Then Owl showed the others how to tie it up with string—to make it stronger against the wind.

"The best way to build a house is with friends who help," said Eeyore. "Thank you!"

"You're welcome," said Pooh. "And now I think it's time for a little something, don't you?"

"But, Pooh, we've been doing 'something' all morning," said Piglet.

Pooh patted his tummy, and said, "Time for something to eat."

Tigger laughed. "Let's bounce over and see what Rabbit's got cooking!" he cried.

They found poor Rabbit slumped in his garden chair, mopping his brow with his handkerchief.

"Rabbit," asked Pooh, "do you have anything good to eat?"

"I've got a whole garden full of vegetables," Rabbit said with a sigh. "But I've been pulling weeds all day, and I'm too tired to pick them."

"May we help?" asked Pooh.

"Did you say 'help'?" asked Rabbit, cheering right up. "Why, yes, that's exactly what I need!"

"Just let me get everything organized," said Rabbit, who suddenly felt quite important and hardly tired at all.

"Pooh, you can pick potatoes, and Piglet, you pick the tomatoes," said Rabbit. "Tigger, you can pick the carrots, if Eeyore will pick the beans. And, Owl, if you would put all the vegetables in the wheelbarrow and bring them to me, I will wash them."

Soon, big, juicy tomatoes, crunchy carrots, and snappy beans covered Rabbit's kitchen counter. The potatoes were cooking in a big pot.

"You have all been so helpful!" cried Rabbit. "To thank you, I want everyone to stay for supper!"

"Mmmmm, yummy," said Pooh.

While Rabbit finished cooking the vegetables, his friends all helped set the table.

"This is the best supper ever," said Pooh.

"A thank-you supper for the best helpers in the Hundred-Acre Wood!" cried Rabbit.

After the meal was over, Pooh and Piglet sat in their Thoughtful Spot for a while and did . . . well . . . they did nothing at all!

"Whew! It feels good to rest," said Pooh.

"Yes," agreed Piglet. "Doing nothing is much more fun after a busy day of helping."